OUTDOOR ADVENTURE

DEEP-SEA FISHING

BY GEORGE PENDERGAST

Gareth Stevens PUBLISHING

HOT TOPICS

Please visit our website, www.garethstevens.com. For a free color catalog of all our high-quality books, call toll free 1-800-542-2595 or fax 1-877-542-2596.

Pendergast, George.
Deep-sea fishing / by George Pendergast.
p. cm. — (Outdoor adventure)
Includes index.
ISBN 978-1-4824-1272-7 (pbk.)
ISBN 978-1-4824-1235-2 (6-pack)
ISBN 978-1-4824-1489-9 (library binding)
1. Big game fishing — Juvenile literature. I. Title.
SH457.5 P46 2015
799.16—d23

First Edition

Published in 2015 by
Gareth Stevens Publishing
111 East 14th Street, Suite 349
New York, NY 10003

Designer: Nick Domiano
Editor: Ryan Nagelhout

Photo credits: Cover, p. 1 Tony Arruza/Photolibrary/Getty Images; cover texture Yuriy Boyko /Shutterstock.com; cover ribbon blinkblink/Shutterstock.com; pp. 4-5 Polka Dot/Thinkstock.com; pp. 6-7 © iStockPhoto.com/richcareys; pp. 8-9 Antonio Balaguer/Thinkstock.com; pp. 10-11 Robert Pernell/Shutterstock.com; pp. 12-13 © iStockPhoto.com/katsgraphics808; pp. 14-15, 18-19, 20-21, 30 (fishing rod) holbox/Shutterstock.com; pp. 21, 30 (life jacket) objectsforall/Shutterstock.com; p. 17 ARENA Creative/Shutterstock.com; pp. 22-23 Natursports/Shutterstock.com; p. 25 Oleg Vinnichenko/Shutterstock.com; pp. 26-27 Susan Quinland-Stringer/Shutterstock.com; pp. 28-29 Leonard Zhukovsky/Shutterstock.com.

Printed in the United States of America

CPSIA compliance information: Batch #CS15GS: For further information contact Gareth Stevens, New York, New York at 1-800-542-2595.

CONTENTS

THE OPEN SEA

Fishing is a great way to relax. Lots of people like to fish from the shore. Some people fish on boats. They like to go deep-sea fishing.

Deep-sea fishing is any kind of fishing done on a boat in water about 100 feet (30 m) or more deep. Many people sail far from land to find deep water with lots of fish in it.

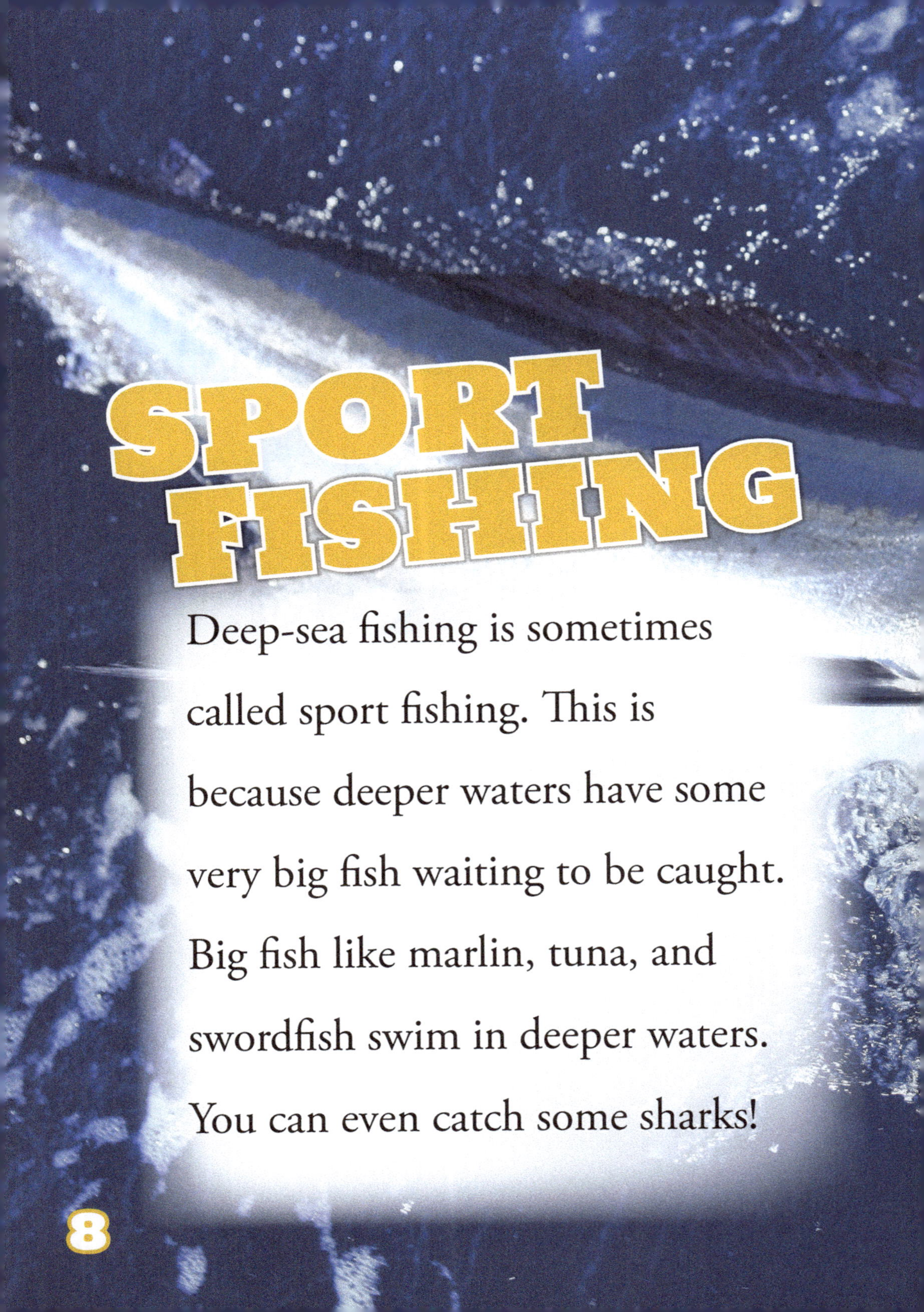

SPORT FISHING

Deep-sea fishing is sometimes called sport fishing. This is because deeper waters have some very big fish waiting to be caught. Big fish like marlin, tuna, and swordfish swim in deeper waters. You can even catch some sharks!

GEARING UP

You need a boat to go deep-sea fishing. Many people pay to take a **charter** boat. Charters have guides to help people learn how to fish safely. Other fishermen have their own boat.

Fishermen use many tools to catch fish. They keep this gear in a **tackle box.** A tackle box holds all the tools a fisherman needs to land a big catch.

ON THE POLE

You can't catch fish without a fishing pole! Deep-sea fishing poles are longer than basic fishing poles. They're made of special metals and are much stronger to help catch big fish.

HOOKS AND BAIT

Fishermen need hooks to catch fish. They put fish food, called **bait**, on the hooks and **cast** a line into the water. The hooks and bait drop deep into the water, where fish take a bite.

Once a fish is on the line, you have to bring it in. Some fish fight for hours! Fishermen may let the fish circle under the boat until it gets tired. Then the line is **reeled** in and is brought on the boat. The fish is caught!

PICTURE TIME

Once the fish is in the boat, it's time to celebrate! Many people take a picture with their catch. Then the fish is put on ice or in a tub to keep it from jumping back into the water!

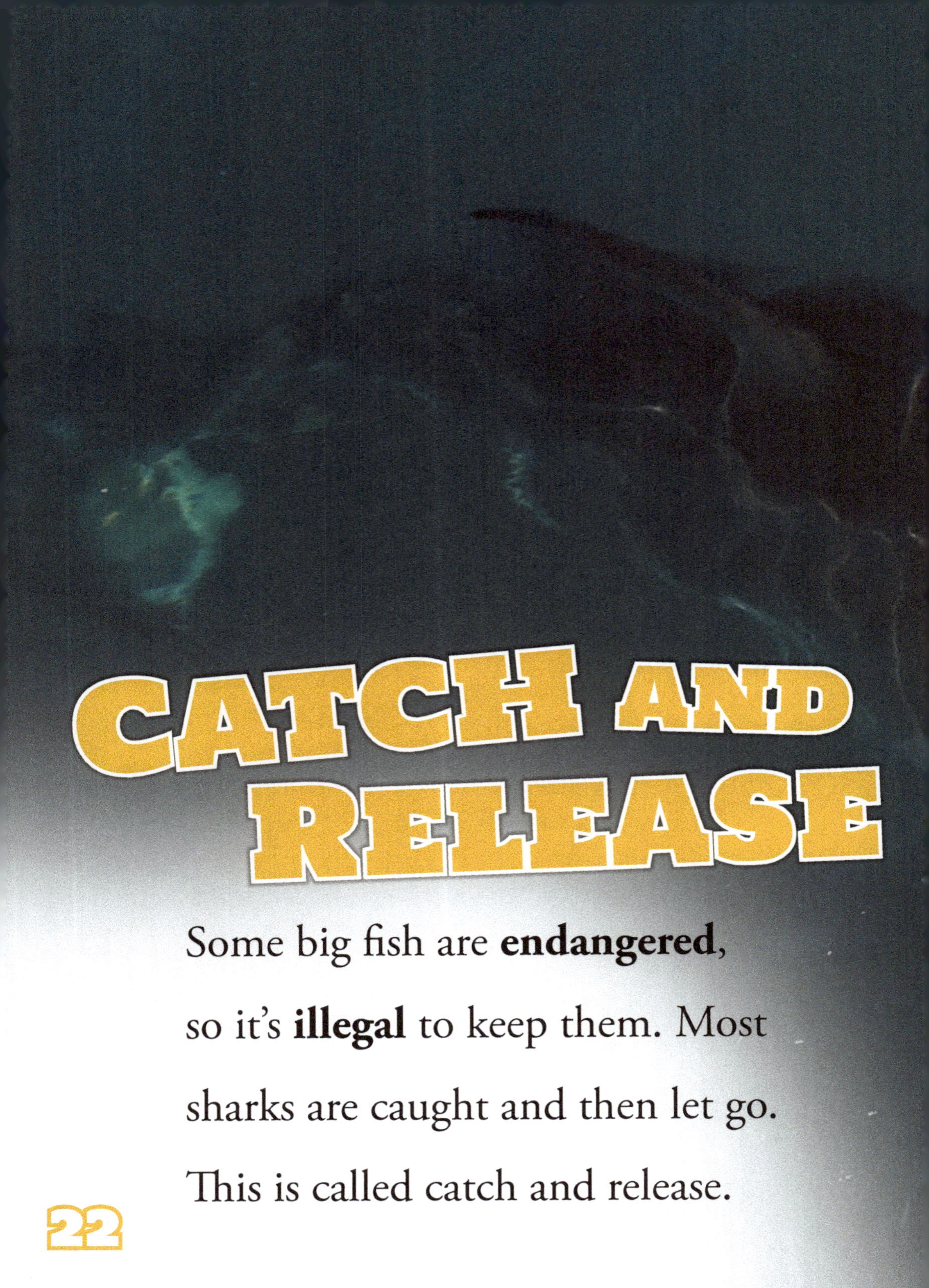

CATCH AND RELEASE

Some big fish are **endangered**, so it's **illegal** to keep them. Most sharks are caught and then let go. This is called catch and release.

CLEAN AND EAT

If you're keeping your fish, you have to clean it. You take the scales off and remove its bones. Then you get the meat ready for cooking.

DON'T GET SICK!

Some people can't handle being on a boat. Their stomach hurts, and sometimes they throw up. On a boat, this is called getting seasick. Some people take medicine to **avoid** being seasick.

HOT SPOTS

There are lots of great places to go deep-sea fishing. People fish year-round in Hawaii and in the Florida gulf. You can even go to Maine to find bluefin tuna or go whale watching! Where will you go fishing?

Deep-Sea Fishing Safety

- Use the buddy system.
- Wear a life vest.
- Don't leave equipment on the ground.
- Be careful with hooks.
- Cast pole away from others.
- Don't cast toward other objects.

FOR MORE INFORMATION

Books

Frazel, Ellen. *Deep Sea Fishing*. Minneapolis, MN: Bellwether Media, 2013.

Gordon, Nick. *Deep Sea Fisherman*. Minneapolis, MN: Bellwether Media, 2013.

Thomas, William. *Deep Sea Fisher*. New York, NY: Marshall Cavendish Benchmark, 2010.

Websites

Deep-Sea Fishing

worldfishingnetwork.com/tips/post/deep-sea-fishing

Learn more about deep-sea fishing with great videos and a how-to guide on this site.

Saltwater Fishing

takemefishing.org/fishing/saltwater-fishing/what-is-saltwater-fishing/

This site has great tips and tricks to help you fish in the ocean.

GLOSSARY

avoid: to stay away from
bait: something used to attract animals
cast: to throw
charter: having to do with a boat you rent for a period of time
endangered: in danger of dying out
illegal: against the law
reel: to bring in a line on a fishing pole
tackle box: a box for storing fishing gear

INDEX